BREYER® Stablemates®

Starlight

By Kristin Earhart
Illustrated by Dan Andreasen

SCHOLASTIC INC.

New York   Toronto   London   Auckland   Sydney
Mexico City   New Delhi   Hong Kong   Buenos Aires

To my niece, Haley–
the next in a long line of horse lovers
– K. J. E.

For Katrina
– D. A.

Library of Congress Cataloging-in-Publication Data

ISBN 13: 978-0-439-72241-4
ISBN 10: 0-439-72241-1

10 9 8 7 6 5 4   08 09 10 11

Printed in the U.S.A.
This edition first printing, October 2008

Table of Contents

Some Good News

One morning, Mr. and Mrs. Clark woke their daughter, Haley, very early.

"There's a surprise in the barn," they told her.

Haley rushed to the barn. She stopped
in front of Midnight's stall. There, Haley
saw a new foal. Midnight licked the foal's
wet coat.

She pushed the foal with her nose,
and the foal stood up.

"Midnight, she's wonderful!" Haley said.
Midnight whinnied happily.

The filly had a black coat like her
mother. And she had a bright white star
on her face.

"What should we name her?" Mr.
Clark asked.

"Starlight," Haley said.

"That's a good name," Mrs. Clark said.

"Starlight will be your horse," Mr. Clark said.

"Thank you!" Haley said. She had always wanted her own horse.

"She will need special care," Mr. Clark said.

"It will be hard work," Mrs. Clark said.

"I can do it," Haley answered. "I know I can!"

Midnight and Starlight

Every day, Haley and her father took care of Starlight and Midnight. They gave the horses water and hay. They took turns cleaning the stall.

Haley watched her father train Midnight. Midnight was a good horse. Midnight did everything that Mr. Clark asked her to do. She stood still when he brushed her. She let him pet her soft nose.

But Starlight was still very young.
And she did not know how to do what
Haley asked.

She did not stand still when Haley
tried to brush her. She did not let Haley
pet her soft nose. Instead, she ran away.

Some days, Haley put the horses out
in the field. Midnight walked and grazed.
But Starlight liked to buck and gallop
around the field.

She also liked to poke her nose around
the fence. There was so much for her to
discover!

When it was time to come in, Haley
called their names. "Midnight, Starlight,"
she yelled.

Midnight always came right away. But
Starlight did not. Haley had to catch her.

Starlight was a lot of work, but she
made Haley laugh. Starlight stole carrots
from Haley's pocket.

Starlight put her nose into everything.
But Starlight still wouldn't come when
Haley called her.

A Whinny of Warning

One night, Haley and her dad heard a loud whinny. They went to the field.

"Midnight," Mr. Clark called.

"Starlight," Haley called.

Midnight came running to Mr. Clark.
She whinnied and whinnied. But where
was Starlight?

Haley and her dad went into the field. There was a hole in the fence. It was just the right size for Starlight to fit through.

"Dad!" Haley cried. "Starlight is gone!"

"Don't worry," Mr. Clark said. "We will find her."

Mr. Clark and Haley looked in the
other fields. They looked in the barn. No
Starlight.

"Where could she be?" Haley asked.
"We haven't looked in the hills,"
Mr. Clark said. "We should go there."

The Dark Hills

A cold wind blew. There were dark clouds in the sky. A storm was coming. Haley followed her dad into the hills.

Haley felt a drop of rain. She heard thunder.

"We will have to turn around soon," Mr. Clark said.

"But, Dad, we can't leave Starlight!" Haley said.

Then Haley looked into the dark night.
She saw something far away. It looked
like a bright star.

Haley made a wish. "Starlight, star bright, first star I see tonight, I wish I may, I wish I might, have my Starlight come back tonight." Just then the star moved!

A high whinny filled the air. The star
came closer.

"Starlight!" Haley called.

Starlight stepped out of the darkness.

She trotted toward Haley.

A True Friendship

Haley ran forward. "Starlight, it's you," she yelled. She threw her arms around the filly.

"Good work, Haley," Mr. Clark said. "Let's take her home."

Soon, they were back in the barn.

Haley's mom was there with Midnight.

"You found Starlight!" Haley's mom said.

"Starlight found us," Haley said. "She heard me call her name."

"She came when you called," Mrs. Clark said. "She is really your horse now."

Haley put Starlight in the stall with
Midnight. Midnight nuzzled her foal.
Mr. Clark fed Midnight a carrot.

Then Starlight pulled a carrot from
Haley's pocket. Haley smiled.

About the Horse

Facts about Morgans:

1. Morgans can be black, brown, bay, or chestnut-colored.

2. All Morgans are descendants of a horse named Figure, born in 1789 in Springfield, Massachusetts. Figure was owned by a teacher named Justin Morgan. Over time, Figure's children became known as Morgans.

3. Morgans are popular competition and show horses, used in English and Western pleasure riding, dressage, and driving.

4. The American Morgan Horse Association is the breed registry for Morgan horses.

5. Two famous Morgan horses carried generals in the Civil War. Rienzi, also known as Winchester, was ridden by Union General Philip Sheridan. Little Sorrel was ridden by Confederate General Thomas "Stonewall" Jackson.

When Horses Are All You Dream About...

It has to be Breyer® model horses!

Breyer® model horses are fun to play with and collect!
Meet horse heroes that you know and love. Learn about horses
from foreign lands. Enjoy crafts and games.
Visit us at **www.breyerhorses.com**
for horse fun that never ends!

Every horse has a story.

READ THEM ALL!

Patch

Belle

Penny

Snowflake

Lucky